This book belongs to
my friend:

A NOTE TO PARENTS

In *Special Delivery*, Oswald has just received a mysterious package. What is inside? Oswald and his friends imagine many things—a pogo stick, a croquet set, and a hot air balloon, to name a few. Like the characters in the story, your child will enjoy using her imagination to guess what is in the box.

As you read through the story, stop as each of Oswald's friends imagines what the box holds. How does each guess reflect that character's personality? Before you reach the end of the book, ask your child what she hopes is in Oswald's box.

Encourage games and activities that foster imagination, which is a very important part of your child's developmental process. For instance, help her act out parts of her favorite books, or take turns, line by line, making up a new story. Fill old pillow-cases or shoeboxes with various objects of different shapes and sizes, then have her try to guess what is inside. You can also fill a basket with old clothes for dress-up fun, and make sure assorted art materials are always available. Whatever the activity, see that your child spends some time alone or with a friend exploring creative play as often as possible.

Learning Fundamental: 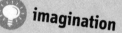 **imagination**

For more parent and kid-friendly activities, go to www.nickjr.com.

SPECIAL DELIVERY

Published by Scholastic Inc., 90 Old Sherman Turnpike, Danbury, CT 06816
SCHOLASTIC and associated logos are trademarks and/or registered trademarks of Scholastic Inc.

ISBN 0-7172-6628-1

Printed in the U.S.A.

First Scholastic Printing, December 2002

SPECIAL DELIVERY

by
Dan Yaccarino

illustrated by
Antoine Guilbaud

SCHOLASTIC INC.

New York Toronto London Auckland Sydney
Mexico City New Delhi Hong Kong Buenos Aires

Oswald the octopus and his pet hot dog, Weenie, were walking home from the post office.

They were very excited about the package they were taking home.

"Gosh, Weenie," said Oswald. "I wonder what this could be!"

"Bark! Bark!" said Weenie.

"Hey there, Oswald!" shouted Daisy. "What's inside your box?"

"I don't know yet," Oswald told her.

"Maybe it's a brand-new pogo stick!" Daisy said excitedly.

She decided to follow Oswald to see what was inside!

"It's good to see you, Oswald!" said Pongo.
"What's inside your box?"
"I don't know yet," Oswald told him.

"Maybe it's a hot air balloon!" Pongo said excitedly.

He decided to follow Oswald to see what was inside!

"Well how-dy-doo, Oswald!" said Cactus Pete and Cactus Polly. "What's inside your box?"

"I don't know yet," Oswald told them.

"Maybe it's shiny new cowboy boots!" Cactus Pete and Cactus Polly said excitedly.

They decided to follow Oswald to see what was inside!

"Good day, Oswald!" said Johnny Snowman.
"What's inside your box?"
"I don't know yet," Oswald told him.

"Maybe it's a great big drum!" Johnny Snowman said excitedly.

He decided to follow Oswald to see what was inside!

"Oh, good morning, Oswald!" said Madame Butterfly.

"Gubba gubba!" said Catrina Caterpillar.

"What's inside your box?" Madame Butterfly asked.

"I don't know yet," Oswald told her.

"Perhaps it's a brand-new tea kettle," she said excitedly.

They decided to follow Oswald to see what was inside!

"Hello there, Oswald," said Andy the Candy Pumpkin. "What's inside your box?"

"I don't know yet," Oswald told him.

"Maybe it's a fancy new yo-yo to do tricks with," Andy said excitedly.

He decided to follow Oswald to see what was inside!

Oswald passed the Egg Twins, Egbert
and his brother, Leo.

"Top of the morning, Oswald!" said Egbert.

"Yes! Yes!" said his brother, Leo. "Tip top!
What's inside your box?"

"I don't know yet," Oswald told them.

"Maybe it's a smashing new croquet set!" the Egg
Twins said excitedly.

They decided to follow Oswald to see what was inside!

"Morning, buddy boy," said Henry.
"Say, what's in the box?"

"I don't know yet," Oswald
told him.

"Maybe it's a brand-new
fishing pole!" Henry said
excitedly.

He decided to follow Oswald to see what was inside.

Finally, Oswald arrived home.

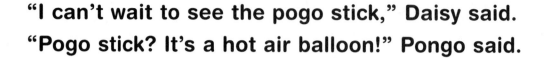

"I can't wait to see the pogo stick," Daisy said.
"Pogo stick? It's a hot air balloon!" Pongo said.

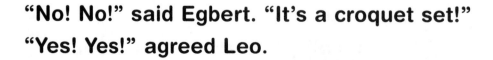

"No! No!" said Egbert. "It's a croquet set!"
"Yes! Yes!" agreed Leo.

"Oswald, what do you think is in the box?"
asked Madame Butterfly.

Oswald thought and thought.

"We can't wait to see what's in the box, Oswald!" Johnny Snowman said.

"Well, let's open it and see!" said Oswald.
"Bark! Bark!" said Weenie.

"Omigosh!" shouted Oswald excitedly.
"It's my new books!"

No one could imagine a more wonderful surprise!